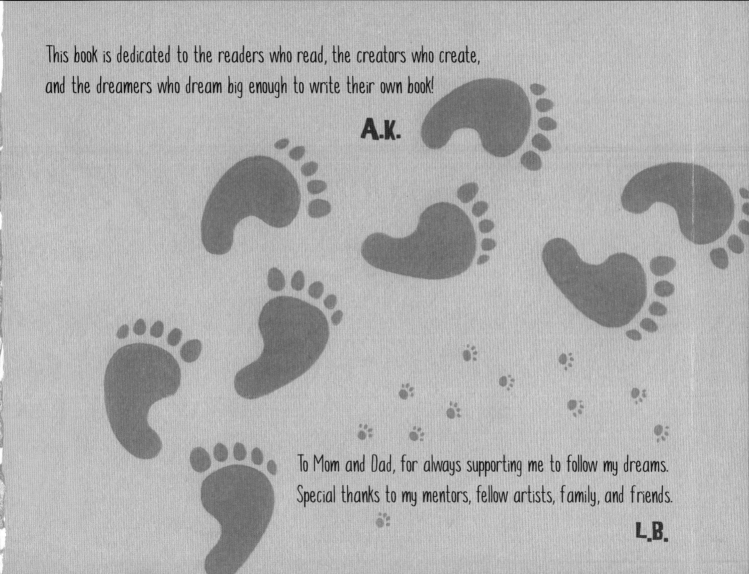

This book is dedicated to the readers who read, the creators who create, and the dreamers who dream big enough to write their own book!

A.K.

To Mom and Dad, for always supporting me to follow my dreams. Special thanks to my mentors, fellow artists, family, and friends.

L.B.

www.mascotbooks.com

For more information, please contact:
Mascot Books
560 Herndon Parkway #120
Herndon, VA 20170
info@mascotbooks.com

Library of Congress Control Number: 2016910984

CPSIA Code: PRTWP0916A
ISBN-13: 978-1-63177-909-1

Printed in Malaysia

Howard
AND THE
WOMPOOPUS

by Allison Krieger • Illustrated by Laura Ballard

I caught a **WOMPOOPUS** today.
I trapped him in my closet
So he would not get away.

I told my friends
And this is what they had to say...

Does he have ears like a fox?

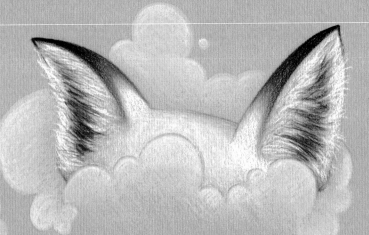

YEP.

And the eyes of a raccoon?

SURE DOES.

Does he have the nose of an otter? **UH-HUH.**

And teeth like a hippo?

EXACTLY.

Does he have hands and feet like a monkey?

JUST LIKE A MONKEY.

And is he the size of a polar bear?

EVEN BIGGER THAN A POLAR BEAR.

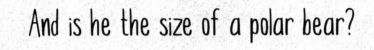

Does he have a tail as long as a leopard's?

NO, his tail is **WAY** longer than a leopard's.

BUT...

My favorite part about him
Is the funny sound he makes.

He sounds kind of like an elephant,
But nothing like a snake.

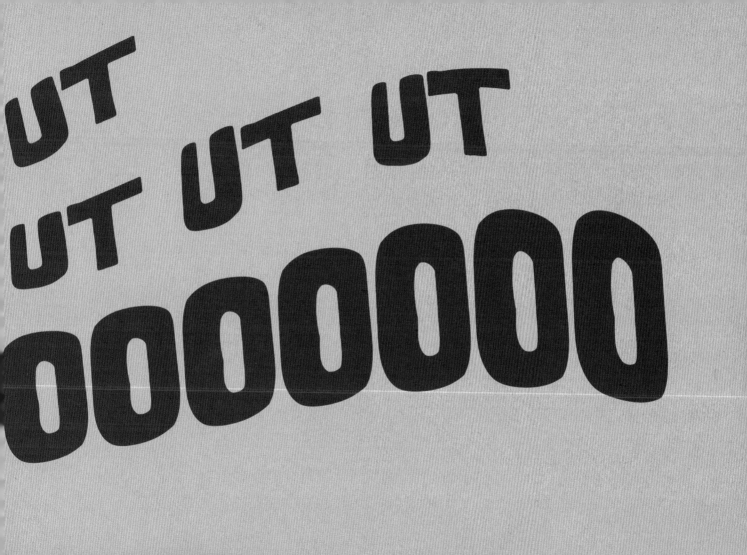

I caught a **WOMPOOPUS** today.
I trapped him in my closet
So he would not get away.

I cannot tell my mother for I know what she would say.

"There is no such thing as a **WOMPOOPUS,** Howard. It's all in your head.

Now close your eyes,
Sweet boy,
AND GO
TO
BED."

About Allison Krieger

When Allison Krieger became a mother, she could not wait to tell her son the original stories her father, Howard, had told her when she was a child. This excitement inspired Allison to write her debut picture book, *Howard and the Wompoopus*, which is based on one of the imaginative characters from those childhood stories. Told from the perspective of a young boy, follow Howard on his adventures in the magical world he creates. Allison hopes this story will do for you what it did for her at such a young age—encourage imagination. Allison currently resides in Issaquah, Washington with her husband and son, and together they hope to continue the tradition by creating more children's books to read to their son and share with you!

About Laura Ballard

Since grade school Laura Ballard wanted to be an artist. Her ability to bring imagination to life has led to illustrating her debut picture book, *Howard and the Wompoopus*! Laura graduated with her BFA in Illustration from Rocky Mountain College of Art + Design and lives in Overland Park, Kansas. To see more of her work, go to lauraballardart.com.